Children's Literature and Illustration Award

ANTHOLOGY

2019

Adelaide Books
New York / Lisbon

ANTHOLOGY 2019
By the WINNERS, SHORTLIST WINNER NOMINEES, AND FINALISTS
of the Adelaide Books Children's Literature and Illustration Award Contest

Cover design by Erin Lee Carman

Published by Adelaide Books, New York / Lisbon
adelaidebooks.org
Editor: Adelaide Franco Nikolic

For any information, please address Adelaide Books
at info@adelaidebooks.org or write to:
Adelaide Books
244 Fifth Ave. Suite D27
New York, NY, 10001

ISBN: 978-1-951214-86-9

Printed in the United States of America

Adelaide Books
Announces the
WINNERS, SHORTLIST WINNER NOMINEES, AND FINALISTS
of the Adelaide Books Children's Literature and Illustration Award,
1st Annual Contest 2019

BEST CHILDREN'S STORY CATEGORY:

The Winner:

Gayle Compton with the story titled ***Roy Raccoon Goes Whale Fishing***

BEST CHILDREN'S ILLUSTRATION CATEGORY:

The Winner:

Erin Lee Carman

BEST CHILDREN'S STORY CATEGORY:

Shortlist Winner Nominees:

Julie Reed with the story titled ***Stella's Umbrellas***

Lazaro Mariano Perez with the story titled ***The Owl's Riddle***

Rita Glen with the story titled ***A Matter of Spelling***

Finalists:

Toni Fuhrman (***The Leftover King***)

Susan L. Pollet (***Juliette Rose's Dream of Becoming***)

Antje Taylor (***Friends Like Taking Turns***)

Carolyn Weisbecker (***Bo and Arrow***)

Robert Holcomb III (***Bennett Clement Jones Bubble Cloud***)

Laura Muncie (***Tiny Mountain***)

Aashi Parikh (***Do Monkeys Cry?***)

Adrian Hardy Hansen (***The Boy With the Inner Voice***)

BEST CHILDREN'S ILLUSTRATION CATEGORY:

Shortlist Winner Nominees:

Tammy Bohlens

Marianne Song

Lisa Wee

Finalists:

Susan L. Pollet

Annaleigha Wilke

Mirela Mandžo

Editor's Note

By Adelaide Franco Nikolic

Being a lover of children's literature, it was a great pleasure to organize the First Adelaide Books Children's Literature and Illustration Award Competition. We received many wonderful submissions and it was a tough job to choose from such a big variety of subjects and styles.

Some submissions made me smile, some made me a bit sad, but in the end, those that brought more joy to my heart were the ones chosen.

In this anthology, you will find what we consider the best. We hope that these stories and illustrations will bring you joy.

Enjoy!

Adelaide

"A childhood without books – that would be no childhood. That would be like being shut out from the enchanted place where you can go and find the rarest kind of joy." (Astrid Lindgren)

Roy Raccoon Goes Whale Fishing

By Gayle Compton

Down the road by the river to the old fishing hole
came young Roy Raccoon with a new cane pole.
He wore a straw hat tipped back at an angle
held fast with green ribbon all in a tangle.
His blue overalls had only one patch.
His bright yellow shirt had stockings to match.
Tied round his neck was a scarf of maroon.
Indeed, he was a most handsome raccoon!

He whistled and sang "How lucky am I
to have gingerbread cookies and blueberry pie,
herring and cake and pink lemonade.
It is easy to see that I have it made,"
sang Roy as he found a nice place in the shade.

"What a swell day for fishing," thought Roy out loud,
"I will take home a catch that will make Mom proud.
With all my good fortune, one never can tell,
I might surprise Mom with a blue-eyed whale!
For a raccoon my size that would be quite a fish.
Yes, a whale would make a remarkable dish!

Just to carry one home a mile or more
would be a perfectly exhausting chore.
The very thought makes me tired as can be.
I must take a short nap for I will catch two or three."

While Roy was napping a fat crow came by
with a huge appetite for blueberry pie,
and also a fondness for herring and cake
and gingerbread cookies—all he could take.
He laughed at poor Roy asleep in the shade.
"A fine meal indeed," said the mean crow with glee
as he hang Roy's hat upside down in a tree.
He laughed so hard he thought he would cry
while Roy dreamed of whales stacked ten miles high!

Roy slept soundly on the soft clover bed
until an acorn struck him quite hard on the head.
"Ouch!" cried Roy, as he awoke in a fright.
"How long have I napped? It is almost night!
I promised Mom I would be home by eight.
My, but it certainly looks mighty late!
My lunch, my lunch! It seems I've been robbed!
No cookies, no pie, no herring, he sobbed.
Who would do such a thing, wondered Roy Raccoon,
a lion, a tiger, or a naughty baboon?"

Soon the forest grew dark—there was only the moon.
"What is that I see?" whispered Roy Raccoon.
"There's a strange looking creature right at my back.
It's long and hairy and bushy and black.
I must run for my life, else I'll be gobbled down whole!"
said Roy as he threw down his new fishing pole.
Was it a tiger, a lion or a wolf on his track?
Poor Roy Raccoon was afraid to look back.

Mr. Fox saw him coming and called from his door,
"What's the hurry, Raccoon?" but it frightened him more.
Presently he stumbled over old Mr. Mole.
"Crazy Raccoon, why don't you watch where you go!"
"Watch out yourself," Roy called out.
"Watch out for the monster with the long hairy snout!"
"Poor Roy," said Mole, rubbing his toes,
"A monster, indeed, with a long hairy nose!"

It was dark in the swamp when he passed Mr. Frog.
"Don't crowd me," he yelled, "I'm being chased by a dog,
or a tiger or lion with a nose like a log.
Get out of my way!" he told Mr. Toad,
"or we both will be eaten. Get out of the road!"

"Help!" cried Roy, nearly frightened to death,
"it is sure to catch me. I'm almost out of breath.
It is getting ready to leap on my back,
this vicious monster all bushy and black."

"Help, save me!" yelled Roy when he saw Mr. Bear.
"I'm being chased by a dragon all covered with hair!"
Bear only chuckled as he gathered some honey.
"That Roy," he thought, "is sure acting funny."

"I can't run much longer. I must find shelter soon.
I want my Mommy," panted Roy Raccoon.

"Mr. Rabbit," pleaded Roy, "please open your door,
I'll be eaten alive. I can't run anymore."

"Go away," said Rabbit, "you silly raccoon.
You are much too fat to fit in my room.
Go see Mrs. Robin. She lives down the way.
Perhaps she wouldn't mind if you stay."

"Mrs. Robin," cried Roy, "I must take a rest.
Won't you please invite me into your nest?"

"Be quiet! My babies are asleep in bed.
They will cry if you wake them. Go away," she said.

"Try Mr. Mouse, down the road half a mile.
He might let you stay for a while."

Faster ran Roy until he spied Mr. Mouse.
"Mouse, Mouse, may I come into your house?"

"Oh no!" said Mouse. "You're too big for my door.
You'd knock down my chimney and break down my floor!
Go see Mr. Turtle. He's a grumpy old guy,
but if I were you I would give him a try."

"Mr. Turtle," begged Roy, "won't you let me inside?
I'm being chased by a goblin and I have nowhere to hide."

"Go away," grumbled Turtle, "you can very well see
there is scarcely room in my house for me!
But I know a lady raccoon who has a nice house
that is too small for a bear and too big for a mouse.
It is just down the road. You should find it real soon.
She must surely have room for a young raccoon."

"Dear me," sighed Roy, "what shall I do?
It won't be long until I'm gobbled in two.
How I wish I had not gone fishing at all."
And he wiped a big tear with his fuzzy paw.

"My, my, said a voice from the edge of the wood,
"all that whimpering and crying will do you no good.
Why, not even a goblin would stay up so late.
Yes, even a monster would be home by eight!"

"Mommy, oh Mommy!" cried Roy, "it's you!
Save me! Save me, or I will be gobbled in two
by lions and tigers and wolves in black,
baboons and monsters and dragons no lack,
and green goblins ready to pounce on my back!"

"Dear me," said Mommy Raccoon to Roy,
"I have never seen such a foolish boy!
There is no need to be frightened, for all is well.
You have been running all night from your own bushy tail!"

Roy was scolded and afterwards fed,
not herring, nor pie, nor sweet gingerbread—
but a cup of bitter bark tea instead,
for he had quite a fever and was sent straight to bed.

After his mommy kissed him and tucked him in tight,
little Roy Raccoon dreamed all night
of baiting his hook with green goblin tails
and catching a hundred blue-eyed whales!

Gayle Compton is an Appalachian writer whose stories and poems for adults have been published widely. "Roy Raccoon Goes Whale Fishing," his first children's story, was written originally for his son Tom. It has been revised for his granddaughter Chloe. Gayle lives with his wife Sharon in Pike County, Kentucky.

Erin Lee Carman is a New York-based designer, printmaker, and self-taught illustrator. Originally from Florida, she moved to New York City in 2016 to pursue an education in sustainable design, and her current focus is on further developing her interests in animation, communication design, and creative management. She is currently doing so in her final year of the B.F.A. Integrated Design program at Parsons School of Design in New York City.

Stella's Umbrellas

By Julie Reed

Her curly hair seldom wears ribbons or bows.
Glasses balance on top of her nose.
She's smart as a whip, funny, petite,
Wears a big crooked grin, cowgirl boots on her feet.

It's delightful to know her. She answers to, "Stella."
In one hand a book, in the other, an umbrella.
She adored her umbrellas, everyone knew.
Having hundreds at home was one rumor that grew.

On days with the summer sun shining so bright,
She'd twirl with one open, no raindrops in sight.
Friends started to wonder. It became quite the query.
Oh, the stories that grew, each one having a theory.

"I think she's a spy, needs to hide, can't be caught."
"They're to shoo bugs away, used to whack, swing and swat."
"She's Queen of Land Lovely, pretending, that's all."
"She needs help to balance, without them she'd fall!"

"Why lug these umbrellas wherever you go?
Please tell us," they asked, "We really MUST know!"
With a nod and a shrug, Stella smiles, bats a wink.
If she shared her big secret, who knows what they'd think.

They aren't mere umbrellas, these posh parasols.
Her balance terrific. Likes bugs, big and small.
What makes them so rare? Why so special…you ask? WELL…
Each umbrella has MAGIC! Each has its own task!

One springs you through air, propelling you high.
Like a kite soaring, with birds you can fly.
There's one that shines sunlight when caught in a storm.
When you start feeling stage fright, one helps you perform.

Afraid of the dark? Hide with covers at night?
Well there's one for that, too! Now you're safe, it's all right.
Say you're playing with friends and it's you they're now seeking,
POOF! You're hidden, camouflaged, just no peeking.

The one with the ruffles can make you feel silly.
Some have pom-poms, ribbons and bows that are frilly.
Use the cheetah print style to run fast in a race.
Ask Mae, her big sister, she came in 1st Place!

It's her Mother that showed her the trick to their twirling.
"You must share a nice thought before spinning and whirling."
Their pop-up has purpose, Stella quite understood.
The magic appears when intentions are good.

To remedy pickles, help friends, bring good cheer.
And that's what she does each day, keeping them near.
So, it happened one day, home from school she was coming.
Her umbrella in tow, she was skipping and humming.

Stella noticed commotion by the pink rosebud tree.
A real ruckus was brewing, so she tiptoed to see.
"Oh, dear!" she gasped when her eyes finally spotted,
"Mean Sid's out to play, trouble's surely been plotted!"

Misjudged by many and feared by most,
Trouble stuck to Sid like jelly to toast.
When she saw his next victim, Stella ran in a hurry.
It was Mac, her kid brother, his eyes filled with worry!

"I need an umbrella! Fast, on the double!"
Only ONE could be opened for this kind of trouble.
She reached in her knapsack; she had to take charge.
This mess needed mending; this dilemma seemed large!

Popping open some magic, she stared in Sid's face,
"Kindly, stop what you're doing, don't cause this disgrace.
You're much bigger than Mac, you surely can see.
We can work this one out. Would you please let him be?"

The crowd became quiet, not one sound to hear.
The birds stopped their chirping; the squirrels hid with fear.
Now, what happened next has this plot take a twist.
Sid stopped, thought a moment, then dropped his clenched fist.

What made Sid soften his grip with such ease??
MAGIC, no doubt, blew in like the breeze.
Stella chose the umbrella that resolved ANY bind.
The words on the handle read, "Always Be Kind."

Squirrels went on to their romping, the kids to their play,
While the birds chirped a song just for Stella that day.
As for Sid? Well, he stopped all his taunting and teasing.
What a magical day. Stella thought and so pleasing!

Each night when Stella gets tucked into bed,
She asks the same question that looms in her head.
"Can umbrellas be magic? Could this really be?
Or does magic come from the goodness in me?"

With a nod and a shrug, Mother winks, shares a smile.
Leaving Stella to question and wonder awhile.
Now the moon's counting sheep, stars twinkle and gleam.
Stella's too tired to think, and drifts off to dream.

In addition to staying home with her three children, **Julie Reed** enjoys her amateur status as a musician and photographer.

Illustration by **Tammy Bohlens**

Tammy Bohlens lives in Hamburg, Germany and studies Illustration at the HAW. She specializes in book illustration and uses traditional ink and dip pen as her mediums of choice, to create imaginative worlds and wondrous atmospheres.

The Owl's Riddle

By Lázaro Mariano Pérez

Zora weaved her way through the crowd.

Her fingers were nimble, flying from pocket to pocket like bees. A copper cowrie here, two silver cowries there … soon she'd have enough money for a decent meal at the *Sleeping Flea. Fried eggs, no, bacon, no, no, roasted beef,* she thought and the thought alone made her mouth water.

She noticed a few people had gathered at the bazaar's board. *A new royal decree.*

"What does it say?" Asked a man with the strong arms only a smith could have.

"I caught the last bit before the herald left. Something about a sizeable reward," said a plump woman. A shopkeeper's wife, Zora decided.

Zora snuck her way in front of the board, quiet as a mouse.

"Can no one among us read?" Lamented the smith, drooping his thick shoulders.

"I can," said Zora, standing on her tippy-toes to read. Her father had taught her.

Everyone looked down at her, then at one another, considering the words for a moment. They burst out laughing soon after. The smith's laugh was deep and hoarse like a snarl; his face reminded Zora of a boar. The fat woman's laugh was more of a croak, her jowls and bulging eyes were those of a frog.

"I hadn't laughed like that in years. You're a funny girl," said the smith, putting a hand on his purse. Some people could tell she was a thief on sight, he was one of them.

"A street urchin that can read, next thing we'll hear about winged pigs," said the woman.

Zora read the decree, raising her voice atop their laughter. "By order of King Orokan Dogo, he who can task His Highness with a riddle he cannot answer, shall be rewarded two hundred golden cowries."

She resumed her march, leaving them to gape at her back.

Her stomach growled. *Two hundred golden cowries.* That much money could keep her belly full for months; she could afford one of those silk dresses that the fancy ladies wore, maybe two. She could even buy herself a winged pig if she so chose. Two hundred. She had never even seen a golden cowrie, let alone two hundred of them together, clinking inside a purse. *That must be what happiness sounds like,* she decided.

But alas, she didn't know any riddles.

Suddenly, she heard a song through the clamor. She couldn't tell why, but the song was familiar to her. She pricked up her ears and followed it past the bazaar. The streets were wide enough for three camels walking side by side and bustling with merchants, moneylenders, jugglers, and beggars. Some parts were cobbled with red bricks while the rest were left bare, so by the time she turned a corner on Madam Naré's Inn, her feet were soiled with red sand and caked in mud. She winced, feeling a blister between her toes. Sandals, she decided sandals would be the first thing she'd buy.

Date palms rose past shops, houses, and the occasional tavern, thread-bare linen awnings hung across rooftops, shading a sea of sun-dried bricks, and the green pyramids dwarfed all of it by hundreds of feet. The Twin Jades. Even from the outskirts of the city she could see them, their golden peaks gleaming in the suns.

Zora found the singer, an old man dressed in flowy rags. Everyone passed by, ignoring his song, but not her. She knew this song well. It came to her that her father sang it often; he was a griot. Snapdragon they called him, after the flower, for he always wore bright-colored robes. She had forgotten a lot about him, but not this song.

"*...a song, the one that brings us closer, a song that does not leave us alone,*" the old man sang, picking at the strings of his lute. His voice was raw and haggard. He wore a red robe, and black pants. He sat on a carpet patterned with owls, resting his back against a dying palm tree. A wide-brimmed straw hat hid his face.

Zora joined him in song. "A song unexpected for my voice..."

"*A song far from death. A song, almost nothing, can do everything,*" they finished in harmony. The last chords resounding in a bittersweet melody.

Zora felt her eyes watering. She put all the money she had stolen that day at the old man's feet. "Thank you," she said, with a thin smile. "You've reminded me of something precious. What's this song called?"

"Why, it doesn't have a name, my sweet child. Folk have been singing it since before I was born." He raised his head to see her. "Such a pretty voice you have. What do they call you, child?"

"Zora. You?"

A cough took him. He looked mal-nourished and sickly. "Well, it's nice to meet you, Zora. I have many names, my friends call me the Owl, and my enemies call me ... well, you don't need to know that name," he said, with a smirk, playing a flamboyant arpeggio on his lute. His eyes were big and black and full of wisdom; they sank beneath eyebrows that were bushy, long, and white. His skin was redder than fire, redder than desert sand, redder than one of the suns that hung in the sky.

The words spilled out of her. "Do you know any riddles?"

"Yes, I know a few. What is weightless, can be seen by the naked eye, and when put in a barrel it makes it lighter?"

Zora chewed on that for a moment, then the answer came to her. "A hole. A hole," she blurted out excitedly.

"That's correct."

If she could guess the answer, then so could the king. She had to go before him with an impossible riddle. "Tell me your best one."

"Yes, I shall, but your money is no good here. The price for this riddle is a tad steeper." He slid the cowries back to her with three bony fingers.

Zora took a step back, remembering something her father had told her, *Owls are an omen of illness and death.* "What are you?"

The man flicked his hat into a tilt. "Why, I'm a griot, advisor to kings and beggars alike. I was born on the crossroads. I come from every land and to every land I must go. I'm the Road, the Owl, the Wanderer, a friend to those with crowns and those without a home alike."

How does he know I'm homeless? Zora decided this owl was not to be trusted. She turned to leave.

"What is weightless yet can crush a man's heart, powerless against the sword yet powerful enough to stop a war, and worth a king's ransom yet a poor man can have it?" The old man strummed his lute as he told the riddle.

She left. *I'll figure out the answer on my own.*

Zora returned to the Owl the next day with two boiled eggs, bacon, and a cup of water.

"It's for you," she said timidly, placing it all on the old man's carpet.

"Eat with me," he said, patting the carpet. "Do you know the answer yet?"

She shook her head, chewing at her lip. She had thought about it hard, but no answer had come.

The days went by and Zora couldn't think of the answer; the old man wouldn't speak of it, but he did teach her songs and jokes and tales about distant lands. He even taught her how to play his five-stringed lute, which she found out was called a xalam.

She heard no one had brought the king a riddle he couldn't answer. In fact, there were rumors that he'd grown annoyed at the last man that went before him and threw him to the dungeons.

Two weeks had gone by when the old man said, "It's time. I'll tell you the answer to my riddle."

She chewed her lip, thinking of all the things she'd buy. "I'd like that."

He smiled weakly at her, then whispered the answer.

Of course. How could she not see it before? It was so simple.

She thanked the Owl and made her way to the palace gates where a long line of bards, griots, and storytellers stood. Most were old bearded men, some were young men, but none were women, and none were children.

The line grew shorter and shorter until night came. Zora was guided to the throne room where the king sat, his head resting on his hand.

"You have a riddle for me," he said, looking amused.

"I do, Your Grace." She made her best impression of a bow. "What is weightless yet can crush a man's heart, powerless against a sword yet powerful enough to stop a war, and worth a king's ransom yet a poor man can have it?"

The king repeated the riddle slowly, looking at her with new interest. He mused on his throne for an hour, then he lurched to his feet. "I have the answer!"

Something twisted in Zora's gut. She didn't want to end up in a dungeon.

"A woman's kiss," said king Orokan.

Zora shook her head.

The suns rose. The king had stayed up all night, thinking and suggesting wrong answers. The servants had brought them courses of food, honeyed chicken, pies, sweet bread. Wine for him and orange juice for her.

Five days went by. Zora had been given many things at the king's orders, a bath came first, three beautiful silk gowns, sleeping quarters at court, and at her request, her very own xalam.

She sprawled on a cushioned chair, playing her xalam, while the king paced by his throne. Black bags had grown under his eyes, his velvet clothes wrinkled, and his bejeweled crown askew.

He raised his finger. "No, no, that's a stupid answer," he chided himself, then shot an icy look at his griot. "Have you nothing to say?"

The griot, who up to that point had been gorging himself on chicken, gulped and squeaked.

"An advisor who can't advise is as useful as hair on a frog. To the dungeons," the king snapped.

Zora frowned. She missed the Owl; the xalam she'd been given, though golden and extravagant, didn't sound half as beautiful as his.

Later on, she went to visit the Owl. She wanted to thank him for everything, but her old friend was gone, only his crooked xalam remained. She found it tucked underneath the fallen branches of the dead palm tree.

Zora picked it up gently. She tuned it and played the nameless song while she walked back to the palace. "*A song, almost nothing, can do everything,*" she sang for everyone and no one, gazing up at the suns.

The king never solved the riddle, and impressed by Zora's wisdom, he made her his new griot.

Lázaro Mariano Pérez was born and raised in Cuba. He moved to the U.S in 2008 and slowly fell in love with writing and telling stories. His Afro-Cuban heritage is a constant influence on his storytelling.

A Matter of Spelling

By Rita Glen

You could say it started with a note. Or maybe a fall from a horse. But really, it all started way back in the fourth grade when The Royal Princess Lucinda decided not to bother about spelling.

At the time, it seemed like a sensible plan. The princess was an excellent student who could read any book in the castle. She could write wonderful stories and poems, better than anyone in her class. So what if they were full of spelling mistakes?

King Stalwart was horrified. "Don't forget you will be Queen one day," he snorted. "A Queen who can't spell is a most ridiculous sight."

Lucinda wasn't at all worried. "A Queen doesn't need to spell," she declared. "I will have my Spellers-in-Waiting check over everything I write."

Queen Abigail sniffed. "If you mean your ladies-in-waiting, they are not hired for their spelling, but to help with your wardrobe. There is no such thing as a Speller-in-Waiting."

"There will be when I'm Queen," laughed Lucinda. "It will be the first of my Great Reforms."

Of course, when word got out about Lucinda's Great Reform, every mother in the land was busily drilling their children in spelling. "You want to wear fine clothes some day? Better take out that spelling list again!" Suddenly the Kingdom was full of perfect spellers.

Except for Lucinda. She was still as kind and polite a princess as anyone could ask, she still excelled in school and fencing and music, but she remained firmly against spelling. She studied hard for History; she labored over French and Spanish, she puzzled over Math, but she refused to waste even a second of her time on her spelling. She accepted her low mark with a gracious smile, like a true princess.

Things continued in this way for some time, until the princess's 16th birthday, when she had a fall from her horse. Lucinda wasn't hurt but the horse ran away, leaving her stranded far from the castle. She was just preparing for a long walk, when a handsome young man rode up.

He was a pleasant looking fellow, riding a white horse and dressed all in silver armor. "A Knight in Shining Armor!" Lucinda thought. "Just what I need!"

Of course, Lucinda should have known that good knights haven't worn silver armor for years. It is a favorite thing of evil knights, trying to hide their wickedness with a bit of shimmer. But Lucinda was so bowled away by Sir Reginald's manners that she forgot this rule.

When Sir Reginald offered to escort her to the castle, Lucinda was thrilled. "How kind," she cooed, picturing the jealous glances of her classmates. "I must reward your bravery. How about a gift of our kingdom's famous lard?"

Now lard is kind of like butter and it is not exactly the thing that you expect from royalty. Lucinda blushed, as she always did when offering this odd gift. She had no choice, however, because lard was the kingdom's official Gift for Minor Acts of Kindness. (Lucinda made a mental note to change this gift as part of her Great Reform.)

Now, the trouble with being a Princess is that everyone knows your flaws. Sir Reginald had heard rumors about Lucinda's spelling problem. He suddenly saw a chance - just a chance - to play a marvelous trick. He looked Princess Lucinda in the eye and beamed.

"What graciousness! I would so love to have some royal lard. Could your Highness possibly write me a note to officially bestow this gift?"

Now, a princess who is a poor speller should be careful about writing notes. But Lucinda didn't think about this detail. She accepted the scroll and ink from Sir Reginald and wrote in her most elaborate handwriting.

"Delightful," said Sir Reginald. "Truly your Majesty is as generous as she is beautiful!"

And so, they rode along, exchanging compliments and remarking on the lovely scenery. When they reached the castle, Lucinda insisted that Sir Reginald be presented to her parents who were equally charmed by his fine manners. They agreed that a gift of lard was a small token for such a gallant knight.

"Lard?" Sir Reginald smiled and coughed delicately. "Hmm, surely your Majesty is in error? Just let me check the note."

And there it was, written down for all to see:

"For his kind deeds, I, Princess Lucinda do give Sir Reginald the best lord in my kingdom."
King Stalwart gasped. "Lucinda, what were you thinking? The best lord in the kingdom - that would be Lord Perfect! How would I explain such a thing to my dear friend?"
"I never promised him a lord!" said Lucinda, stamping her feet. "I already told you. He asked for lard. I just misspelled it!"

But Sir Reginald kept waving the piece of paper and insisting on his present. The King had to think quickly. He suddenly remembered an ancient (and very sensible) law against giving people as gifts. Sir Reginald's request was simply illegal. He would have to ask for something else, a fine sword, a noble steed, perhaps a bag of gold? Something more appropriate.

"Very well," said Sir Reginald, smiling evilly. "I need some time to think about a suitable gift though. I shall meet with the princess tomorrow - alone - in the center of the Great Hall. Don't forget your scroll and pen, Princess. A written request can only be cancelled by another written request!"

And, with that, Sir Reginald rode grandly away. The King and Queen were dismayed. With Lucinda's spelling, it would be impossible to predict what they could lose the next day. There was only one thing to do. Lucinda must study spelling as she had never studied before.

Lord Perfect drew up a list of possible words that could be her downfall. "Put 'kingdom' on it," suggested the King. "Don't forget 'castle' and "jewels," said the Queen. Lucinda sat meekly, from time to time suggesting a few of her favorite possessions like "Hound," her falcon and "Dashy" her kitten. Then she set to work, doing the first real studying that she had ever done.

If you've ever studied for a hard spelling test, you know something of what Lucinda went through. But, unless you've never studied for any spelling test, you can't really understand how hard it was for Lucinda.

By noon the next day, Lucinda was filled to the brim with royal words. She walked confidently into the Great Hall where Sir Reginald was waiting.

What a sight! The castle servants had been busy all night too. The Great Hall tapestries had all been changed. Every scene contained as many royal words as possible, embroidered tactfully over the appropriate object. Everyone in the castle was clustered around the edges of the Great Hall to watch Lucinda write out her bequest. They all cheered when she arrived. "Yay, Princess Lucinda!" they called, "You can do it!" Lucinda smiled back, blushing a little because each person had their job or title embroidered on their clothing.

Lord Perfect coughed gently, "Ahem, ah, it was such an important duel, your Majesty.... ah, I took the liberty of ordering new court uniforms."

"Wonderful idea!" King Stalwart agreed enthusiastically. "As a matter of fact, I had a new crown made up myself. Don't want that awful Knight to see us looking shoddy!"

The new crown was a beautiful sight, glittering with gold and encrusted with jewels. It had "CROWN" clearly spelled out on the rim with emeralds. Lucinda blushed furiously, but it was no time to get indignant. Sir Reginald was already waiting in the center of the room, lurking near the parchments and inks.

Queen Abigail kissed Lucinda fondly. "Do your best, dear, and don't forget, 'i' before 'e', except after 'c'."

"Keep spelling 'kingdom' over and over to yourself," King Stalwart added. "And remember, a vowel is like a vassal. Handle them firmly and fairly and they will serve you loyally. Mistreat them and they can be treacherous!"

Lucinda walked to the center table, feeling that every eye was upon her. Sir Reginald looked just as gallant as ever. "Don't worry, Princess," he assured her smoothly, "I only have a simple request. I feel so bad about my greediness yesterday. If you will only give me your best horse, I will feel amply rewarded."

"Rats!" thought Lucinda, "I studied all those royal words for nothing! What a waste of time!" But she was still relieved. Her best horse was a dignified old mare, only used for state occasions. Lucinda had been wanting a more spirited mount for some time now. She grabbed the piece of paper and scribbled quickly before the Knight could change his mind. She smiled as she imagined the cheer that would ring up from her subjects when Lord Perfect read the scroll aloud.

"Charming," said Sir Reginald, "I am overcome with your graciousness." He smiled slyly and handed the parchment to a nearby page, who carried it across the room to Lord Perfect. The Great Hall went silent as doom.

Lord Perfect unrolled the scroll and read loud and clear:

"For his kind deeds, I, Princess Lucinda do give Sir Reginald my best house."

The entire Hall erupted in shocked gasps and whispers. Too late, Lucinda realized her error. The King and Queen rushed over to examine the scroll.

"Your best house!" King Stalwart simply couldn't believe it. "Are you aware that would be the castle? Where are we supposed to live?"

Lucinda blushed bright red. "I'm so sorry, Father," she stammered. "He asked for my best horse. It was those treacherous vowels."

The King looked pleadingly at Sir Reginald, but he just smiled his smooth smile. "A bargain is a bargain. There it is written down in the Princess' own hand."

There was a shocked silence as the Queen mentally packed suitcases in her mind. The King was calculating how many troops he would need to hold the castle. Only Lucinda kept her wits about her.

"What a clever fellow you are!" she cooed. "And so handsome too! I think that I have finally met a man smart enough for a princess. Perhaps you would give up the house in exchange for a kingdom?"

"Really?", said the Knight.

"Why not?", asked Lucinda. "One man is as good as any other, and I would like my parents to keep their home. Give me a pen and parchment and I will seal the bargain on the spot."

It was brought, very hesitatingly by Lord Perfect. Sir Reginald could hardly believe his good fortune. Marry the princess? It was beyond belief.

The King and Queen just looked at each other glumly. They knew they couldn't change Lucinda's mind. They'd never persuaded her of anything, why would they succeed now?

Lucinda took up her pen, wrote firmly on the parchment and handed it to Lord Perfect.

Sir Reginald beamed smugly as Lord Perfect read aloud.

"For his kind deeds, I, Princess Lucinda do give Sir Reginald my hound in marriage."

Lucinda grinned from ear to ear as the Great Hall exploded into cheers and whistles. Sir Reginald was enraged! "What's going on here? That's not what you said, just now!"

"I can't remember," said Lucinda grandly. "I only know that a promise in writing can only be cancelled by another promise in writing."

Lucinda looked slowly around the room at her future subjects. "And now, I am off to the high tower. A princess should definitely be able to spell - and I have a lot of work to do!

Rita Glen is an elementary teacher from Lunenburg, Nova Scotia. She enjoys writing with children, particularly watching their confidence grow as they share their stories with others. Much of her own writing is inspired by the interests and observations of her community of child writers.

Illustration by **Marianne Song**

Marianne Song is an essayist who strives to reproduce the feelings and memories with poetic images through English instead of her mother tongue, Korean to convey her raw emotions as honestly as possible, otherwise might be fabricated by self-consciousness.. The way she explores her experiences and memories to correlate with social issues corroborate her viewpoint that arts can be far away from reality. Her education in Switzerland and China expanded her capacity of cultural tolerance arising from different ethnics. A variety of people she met, talked to, and shared her feelings with in two countries were well-melt into her memoir. Currently, she is working as a writer and English instructor in Jeju Island, Korea with an unwavering belief that someday her angst and hardships could be transformed into artistic treasure in the same way the natural wonders of Jeju were made from volcanic eruption. Whenever facing a big challenge, she quietly whispers to herself 'Don't be afraid, follow your heart.'

The Leftover King

by Toni Fuhrman

Once upon a time there was a handsome young King who loved to eat leftovers.

It was partly because he didn't like to waste good food, and partly because there were so many hours between breakfast, lunch, and dinner. And even more hours between dinner and breakfast.

He was often seen in the kitchen or pantries of his castle, heaping a tray with slices of mutton, ham, slabs of pigeon pie, pickles, cheese, biscuits, apples, plums, cookies shaped like tiny castles, and gingerbread men.

His tray piled high; he would climb the winding back stairs that led to the Royal Chambers.

The King's Royal Chef and the Sous Chef (who was as small as the Royal Chef was big) stayed out of sight. The kitchen staff looked the other way or pretended they didn't see him.

At feasts and banquets, the King was sometimes seen tucking lumpy napkins deep within the folds of his royal robe.

The lovely young Queen tried not to make a fuss, because she loved the King, and the leftovers were very tasty.

Their son, the little Prince, liked to eat leftovers with his parents. He clapped his hands in delight when he was brought to the Royal Chambers, and wailed when the servants, or the Royal Tutor, took him away.

Sometimes the King, the Queen, and the little Prince ate leftovers together in the King-Sized Royal Bed.

★

One day, the King ordered all of his Knights and Ministers to meet at the castle in one week's time. They were to discuss important matters of state, and then have a great feast.

The big day came. The Royal Master of Ceremonies announced the Knights and Ministers, one by one, as they arrived. They included the Knights of the White Horse, the Minister of the Castle Interior, the Minister of Drawbridges, Moats, and Turrets, the Minister of Myth and Magic, and the Minister of the Defenseless. The meeting began in the Great Assembly Room.

The King laid out his plan: to help the poorest of his subjects, to find work for men and women who could not find jobs, to take care of the old people when they were sick or could no longer work, and to tax the richest of his subjects.

Most of the Knights and Ministers nodded their heads and said, "Yes!" and "Jolly good!" when they heard the King's plan.

There were, however, a few Naysayers, who kept interrupting the meeting, shouting, "Nay! Nay!" whenever they heard, "Tax the rich" or "Feed the poor."

After a long time, the King put a stop to the shouting and ordered that a vote be taken. The Naysayers lost the vote. The King's plan was accepted and made the law of the land.

It was time to eat and celebrate.

The King and his family sat at the head table in the Great Hall. His guests sat at long tables on either side of the head table.

Everyone was happy—except, of course, for the Naysayers.

The Royal Priest gave thanks, and the feast began.

The meal went on for a long time. The guests were hungry, and the food was good.

The Under-the-Table Dogs panted with joy as delicious scraps of food fell on the floor or were tossed to them.

The King tucked a few lumpy napkins beneath his royal robe, but his guests didn't notice, or politely looked away.

At last the feast came to an end. The King stood up. Everyone turned to face him. In his magnificent red velvet robe, the King had never looked so handsome or so majestic.

Then the King flung up his arms in a victory salute. As he lowered his arms, the red velvet robe slipped from the solid gold clasps that fastened it together and slid to the floor.

There he stood—a King clad only in his red woolen long johns (for castles are very cold), and a full-length apron with row upon row of pockets, from his chest to his knees.

Many of the pockets were bulging with food from the feast.

Everyone gasped. Then there was a hush as those seated at the tables stared at the King. No one moved or spoke, except for the little Prince, who clapped his hands and laughed.

The King's apron was, indeed, cleverly made to hold leftovers. There were large bulky pockets for chicken legs, flat pockets for slices of ham and mutton, puffy pockets for fruit and tarts, and smaller pockets for chunks of cheese and bread.

All of the pockets were lined with silk so that the leftovers did not stain the royal robe.

After a long silence—a silence that seemed as long as the Hundred Days' Rain to everyone present—the King lifted his chin, pulled his shoulders back, and tucked his right thumb into one of the pockets of his apron—dislodging a plump chicken leg.

"Behold," he said, "my new invention!"

The guests looked at each other and waited. The King went on:

"Why should we waste good food, throw it to the dogs at our feet, when there are so many children, old people sick in their beds, men and women shivering with cold and hunger, in bare shelters within a mile of where we sit and eat? Why, indeed, did we have this Assembly, if not to find ways to help them?"

The King continued, with great solemnity:

"I hereby proclaim that every Knight and Minister in my Kingdom shall wear an apron for leftovers at the dinner table, twice a week, as well as on Sundays and feast days. You will give the leftovers to the poor and needy."

He paused. The Great Hall was as quiet as a church.

"I would not object," said the King, "if you were to eat some of the leftovers yourselves."

Then he stood very tall. Even in his long johns and apron, he looked like a king.

"In conclusion," he said, "know this: I don't want anyone in my Kingdom to be hungry!"

The silence continued for a few moments.

Then everyone—except, of course, for the Naysayers—began to clap their hands and shout, "Hoorah!"

The little Prince shouted, "Hoorah! Hoorah!"

The Under-the-Table Dogs barked and howled.

And so it was.

The Royal Wardrobe Master was put to work the next morning preparing apron patterns for everyday wear, holidays, and royal occasions.

Everyone scrambled to be among the first to put in his or her order for an apron.

Before long, children all over the Kingdom began to look healthier. The old people were happier. A group of the poorest men and women got back their strength, found jobs, and formed a union.

The King continued to visit the kitchen and the pantries. But instead of hiding, or turning their backs to him, the Royal Chef, the Sous Chef, and the kitchen staff smiled and curtseyed, and went on with their work.

Some made their own copies of the apron.

After "The Feast of the Apron"—as it came to be known—the little Prince used his apron to feed the Under-the-Table Dogs. The dogs had been looking leaner since that great event.

And "The Leftover King"—as he came to be known—the Queen, the little Prince, and everyone in their well-fed Kingdom, lived happily ever after.

Toni Fuhrman is the author of three novels, including A Windless Place, published by Adelaide Books. Her short story, "Water Moon," was included in the Adelaide Literary Award Anthology: Best of 2017. Toni lives in Los Angeles and enjoys writing stories for children as well as adults. Her personal essays on writing and reading are at tonifuhrman.com.

Juliette Rose's Dream of Becoming

by Susan L. Pollet

I have a dream, that when I grow up, I will be . . .

Adventuresome like Amelia Earhart, the first female pilot to fly across the Indian Ocean.

Articulate like Anne Frank, a young Jewish girl, who wrote a diary while hiding from the Nazis during World War II.

Artistic like Georgia O'Keefe, an inventor of modern art.

Athletic like Serena Williams, a tennis champion.

Beautiful in body and soul like Maya Angelou, a poet, singer, memoirist and civil rights activist.

Brave like Ida Lewis, a lighthouse keeper, noted for her heroism in rescuing people from the seas.

Champion for human rights like Eleanor Roosevelt, the longest serving First Lady of the United States.

Compassionate like Florence Nightingale, the founder of modern nursing.

Confident like Madame Curie, a scientist, and first woman Nobel Prize winner.

Determined like Rosa Parks, the mother of the modern freedom movement, who participated in bus boycotts.

Disciplined like Honorable Ruth Bader Ginsburg, a brilliant lawyer and hardworking United States Supreme Court Justice.

Exploring like Sacagawea, who participated in an expedition of the Louisiana Territory.

Forward thinking like Gloria Steinem, a spokesperson for the feminist movement.

Funny like Carol Burnett, a comedian, actress, singer a writer, best known for her television comedy show.

Graceful like Misty Copeland, the first African American woman to be promoted to principal ballet dancer.

Generous like Melinda Gates, the co-founder of the world's largest private charitable organization.

Honest like Sandra Day O'Connor, the first woman to serve on the United States Supreme Court.

Kind like Oprah Winfrey, the media mogul, best known for her successful talk show, and as an influencer.

Leading like Susan B. Anthony, who helped to obtain the right to vote for women.

Patient like Anne Sullivan, a teacher and life-long companion of Helen Keller, her blind and deaf student.

Persistent like Hillary Clinton, a lawyer, First Lady, Secretary of State, United States Senator and Presidential candidate.

Pioneering like Dr. Elizabeth Blackwell, the first woman to receive a medical degree in the United States.

Poetic like Emily Dickinson, one of America's greatest and most original poets.

Prolific like Louisa May Alcott, a bestselling author of her time.

Selfless like Mother Teresa, a nun and missionary, who devoted her life to caring for the poor and sick.

Song filled like Idina Menzel, an actress, singer and songwriter.

Tough like Golda Meir, a former Prime Minister of Israel.

If I do not grow up to have all of these traits, I dream of accepting all that I become. I dream of being filled with joy and laughter, and with love for my brother William, for all of my family, and for the world community of women and men.

Illustration by **Susan L. Pollet**

Susan L. Pollet resides in New York City, and loves to write, to make art, to travel, and to have adventures. She has a life partner, several daughters and a grandson and a granddaughter. In 2019 her book "*Lessons in Survival: All About Amos*" was published by Adelaide Publishing. In 2018, Susan was the Shortlist Winner of the Adelaide Literary Award. Susan has been a lawyer for forty years, primarily in the area of family law. Ms. Pollet is a 1979 graduate of Emory University School of Law and a 1976 graduate of Cornell University. She graduated as a member of two honorary societies, and has published over sixty articles on varied legal topics in the New York Law Journal and law reviews in the area of family, criminal and domestic violence law. She has participated in multiple legal education training programs as an organizer, speaker and moderator, and taught college law courses. Susan has been active in the women's movement for decades as a chair of multiple committees and as President of the Westchester Women's Bar Association ("WWBA"), and as Vice President of the Women's Bar Association of the State of New York. Ms. Pollet is a recipient of the Joseph F. Gagliardi Award for Excellence, given to a non-judicial employee of the Unified Court System in the Ninth Judicial District for "distinguished service, devotion to duty and the administration of justice, and for outstanding service to the public." She is a recipient of the Marilyn Menge Award for Service, given to a member of the Women's Bar Association of the State of New York for "valuable and significant contributions to a chapter or to the statewide organization." She also served as Executive Director of Pace Women's Justice Center, whose mission is to eradicate domestic violence and to further the legal rights of women, children and the elderly through the skillful and innovative use of the law. She served as the Director of the New York State Parent Education and Awareness Program, which was designed to help separating or divorcing parents better understand the effects of their breakup on their children and to give them information and ideas about how to make the new family situation easier and more livable for themselves and their children. She worked on special projects for the Office of Court Administration. She also served as a lawyer for children, a court attorney to a judge, and as a prosecutor and a grants administrator. For the past eighteen years she has been the Archive and Historian Chair for the WWBA, which includes providing a monthly interview in its newsletter of judges and lawyers. She has a strong desire to provide the public with information about interesting people's lives who give us all hope. *Lessons in Survival: All About Amos* continues her work in that vein.

Friends Like Taking Turns

by Antje Taylor

Lap, the little dinosaur, is playing in the grass, when his best friend Pit comes running up to him.

'Lap, what are you doing?' asks Pit.
'I have found this stick, which is great for throwing and catching,' replies Lap.

'Can I see?' asks Pit excitedly. 'Yes, but you can only look,' Lap tells Pit and he holds out the stick for her to see.

'But I want to try it,' says Pit and she tries to grab the stick from Lap. 'No, it is mine,' shouts Lap and he pulls on the stick himself.

Both little dinosaurs start pulling on the stick, until ....Crack.... the stick breaks.

'Oh no,' cries Lap, looking at the two pieces of the stick.

'You broke it, Pit!' says Lap. 'No, you did' responds Pit.

'What is the matter?' asks Mummy Dinosaur, coming over to the two little dinosaurs.

'Pit has broken my playing stick,' exclaims Lap. 'No, I have not,' shouts Pit. 'I just wanted to play with it too.'

'But it is mine,' roars Lap, 'you can't have it.'

'Lap,' says Mummy Dinosaur, 'wouldn't it be more fun if Pit played with you?'
'But, Mummy, it is my stick!'

'Why don't you throw the stick for Pit to catch and then she can do the same?' suggests Mummy Dinosaur. 'You can take turns.'

Lap looks first at the broken stick and then at Pit. 'Playing with Pit is more fun than by myself,' thinks Lap.

'Okay,' smiles Lap. 'Catch, Pit' he shouts and throws the stick.

Lap and Pit play all day long together, taking turns throwing and catching the stick.

Antje Taylor was born and raised in Germany. She moved to Australia over ten years ago and now lives in Brisbane with her husband Craig and her two young children, Lars and Pip. When she is not a mum, Antje works as a management consultant. She enjoys travelling, outrigger canoeing, spending time on the beach and reading books, both for herself or to her children. She has published her first children's book "Friends don't like roaring" this year and has enjoyed the joy it brings to her own children, but also others.

Bo and Arrow

by Carolyn Weisbecker

Bo scowled as he dug the toe of his shoe into the soft dirt. "Come on, Axel, let me come with you."

Brother Axel, at age 12, was older than Bo by three years, a fact he taunted Bo about whenever he could, which was often. He slightly turned but kept walking. "Why do you keep hanging around me? Go help Mom or something." He turned back around. "You're like a flea on a dog, Bo. Tiny and annoying."

"Wait!" Bo's voice sliced through the quiet morning like a bolt of lightning. He stood on his tiptoes to look taller. "I can get the ball for you whenever it goes over the fence. I can carry the bats. I can—"

"No, you can't. You're just a baby." Axel's long legs broke into a run at the sight of his friends. "Hey, guys, do you want my baby brother hanging around us today?"

The boys howled and grunted like a pack of angry wolves. Their words floated over Bo like heavy rain clouds. He pushed his blue cap down toward his eyes. "Tell your friends to stop teasing me." He stuck out his lip. "Or, I'll tell Mom."

Axel brushed a strand of sweaty hair away from his forehead. "Go ahead. That's what babies do."

Bo's shoulders slumped as he watched the boys gather on the ballfield. I wish I had a friend right now. Then his brown eyes opened wide. "Dillon! Hey, Dillon, wait up!"

His classmate, Dillon, stopped. He pushed his wire-framed glasses higher on his nose. "What's up, Bo? I thought you had taekwondo this morning."

"Not today. We've got scorpions, so Master Ke is spraying the building." He grinned. "He says they're in the locker room. Wish I could see them."

"Yeah. Me, too." Dillon began walking again, only faster. Bo hurried to catch up with him. "I can't hang out today, Bo. I'm going over to my cousin's house."

"Can I could come with you?"

"Sorry. His mom only lets him have one friend over at a time."

Bo's mouth fell open. "Maybe if I come with you, she'll change her mind."

"I don't think so," Dillon said. "I'll see you tomorrow."

Bo watched Dillon cross the street; his body got smaller and smaller until he was gone. He filled his lungs and exhaled a gush of air. I wish I had a friend right now, he thought.

"Bo, wait up!"

He grinned as a girl skipped over to him. "Hey, Grace!"

Grace was his neighbor. She played with a clip that held back her red hair. "I'm going for ice cream. Where are you going?"

"Home, I guess."

"Why don't you come with me? We can split a cone."

Bo smacked his lips and nodded.

But then he heard another voice, and his face dropped. Another girl joined him, but Bo didn't know her.

"What're you doing here, Grace? I thought you had dance class this morning."

"Hi, Clare. I didn't feel like going today," Grace said. "Do you want to hang out with us?"

Clare wrinkled her nose. "Is he coming?"

Bo gulped and looked at Grace. "She invited me."

"Sorry, Bo, but Clare is here now," Grace said. "We're best friends."

I wish I had a friend right now, he thought. Bo's head dropped as the two girls wandered away. He stooped down, grabbed a pebble, and threw it. A flash of gray flew out of the bushes.

He stepped back but stumbled over the curb. Wincing, he scrambled to stand to face his attacker. "You almost killed me!"

A gray-striped cat stood at his feet. At the sound of Bo's voice, he arched his back and puffed out his tail.

Bo knelt down and held out his hand. "You're pretty tough for a dumb cat. Come here, I won't hurt you."

The cat remained frozen.

"You flew outta that bush like an arrow. Come on, let me pet you."

The cat sniffed Bo's hand. Then he rubbed his head against it and purred.

Bo laughed. "Hey, that tickles." He stood. "I'm going home now, so don't follow me."

As he strode down the sidewalk, Bo paused to rub the cat behind the ears every time he saw a stop sign. When he finally reached his house, he saw his mother watering her plants.

"Hi, Bo. Those darn squirrels are still digging in my garden. I wish I knew how to keep them out." Mom groaned. "What's that cat doing here?"

"I told him to stop following me, but he wouldn't listen."

"He looks like a stray. I'll call the animal shelter."

Bo picked the cat up. "If he's a stray, can we keep him?"

"I'm sorry, Bo. We don't have room for another pet."

"But all we have is an aquarium and Axel's mouse. Those aren't pets."

A muscle in Mom's jaw twitched. "We can't keep him, but you can give him something to eat while I call the shelter."

"I always wanted a cat," Bo nuzzled his chin against the cat's head. "I'll take care of him all by myself, Mom. Please?"

"I'm not changing my mind, but we can give him some of the leftover ham from last night," Mom said.

Bo followed his mother into the kitchen. He pulled the ham out of the refrigerator and filled a bowl with water. "Poor hungry, lonely cat. He could be my friend."

"I told you we can't keep him," Mom said. "Besides, he might already have a family."

"Yeah, right." Bo watched the cat eat, then Bo carried him outside. "I bet if Mom thought you were useful, she'd let you stay."

The cat purred as he lifted a paw to clean his face.

Bo rubbed his head to think. "Hey, Mom!"

"What is it, Bo?"

"You've got to see this," he said. "Follow me!"

Bo's mother followed him as he scooped up the cat and rushed toward the shed.

"I saw this huge snake in here last night, and I was afraid to catch him, but I bet Arrow can." Bo pulled the door open and set the cat inside. "Go get him, Arrow!"

"Really, Bo? Since when are you afraid of snakes? And, why are you calling him Arrow?"

Bo thought about how the cat surprised him by rushing out of the bushes. "Because he's as fast as an arrow. He'll catch that snake in no time." They waited as Arrow inched toward the snake. The snake didn't like it.

"Hisss!"

Bo's mom laughed as Arrow bolted for the door. "That explains why he's so thin."

"You should've told me you're afraid of snakes, Arrow." Bo coaxed the cat out from under the car. Maybe Arrow's hunting instincts will kick in if he saw a mouse, he thought. Bo raced to Axel's room where he kept his pet mouse, Sam. He grabbed Sam from his cage. "Sorry, Sam, no hard feelings. Arrow? Here kitty, kitty!"

Arrow had followed him. He sat in the doorway. "Meow.

"I have another idea that will make Mom like you. Just act like you're angry with this mouse." Bo knelt down with the mouse so the cat could sniff him. "Mom, come here! Look what Arrow did!"

Seconds later, Bo looked up at his Mom. "Now what, Bo?"

"Arrow caught this mouse. Isn't he a good hunter?"

His mother frowned at the mouse in Bo's hand. "Isn't that your brother's mouse?"

Bo shrugged.

"Give it to me." She cupped the mouse in her hands and sighed. "This is Axel's mouse. Bo, stop playing games with this cat."

Bo sat down on the porch step with Arrow by his side.

"We've only got one more chance to get Mom to change her mind," Bo said. He glanced around the yard. Then he saw a squirrel perched on a branch in their tree. He jumped up, rushed to the tree, and pushed Arrow onto one of the low branches. "Go ahead and climb up. I'll tell Mom you've cornered a squirrel. That will impress her."

Arrow stood frozen on the branch. Bo winked at him. "Mom, come here! You have to see this!"

Mom marched through the backdoor, a towel in her hand. "Now what?"

Bo pointed. "Arrow chased a squirrel up that tree. I bet it's the same one that keeps digging in your garden."

"Meow, meow, meow!"

Bo's mother shook her head as Arrow paced the length of the branch. "What a fraidy-cat!"

He reached up and pulled the crying cat into his arms. "It's okay. I've got you, Arrow."

Mom reached into her pocket and pulled out her cellphone. "Wonder who that is?"

While Mom answered her phone, Bo buried his face in Arrow's gray fur. "I'm sorry. I tried."

Mom shoved the phone back in her pocket. "That was the animal shelter. They can't pick him up until tomorrow morning, so he can stay for the night."

"Yes!"

"Now, Bo, he's leaving in the morning. You understand that. Right?"

He nodded as Axel strolled into view. "Oh, great. Looks like Bo's got that stupid cat that hangs around the ballfield."

"Do you know who he belongs to?" Mom asked.

"Sure. It belonged to old Mrs. Lewis from down the street. Remember? She moved to California a few months ago to live with her daughter."

Bo stepped closer to his mom. He held Arrow up. "Isn't that sad, Mom? Look how unhappy Arrow looks."

Axel looked from the cat to his mother. "Please tell me we're not keeping that grungy cat, Mom."

Bo ignored him. He set Arrow down, pulled out his shoelace, and dangled it above Arrow's head. "Look how playful he is, Mom."

Mom rolled her eyes. That evening, Bo pulled the shoelace across the floor while Arrow stalked, pounced, and swatted it.

"It's time to put that cat in the basement and get to bed," Mom said.

Bo rubbed his eyes. "Thanks for letting him spend the night. I had the best day ever."

"You're welcome, honey. Make sure you shut the basement door. I don't want that cat wandering around."

Bo swooped the cat up then stopped at the basement door. He sat Arrow down on the top step then gave the door a gentle nudge. "Goodnight, Mom!"

"Sweet dreams, Bo."

As Bo bounded up the steps to his room, Mom went into the kitchen and returned with a cup of tea. After setting her cup down, she flopped into her favorite chair and reached for her knitting basket. It slipped from her hand, and a ball of yarn tumbled out. A flash of gray rushed out from behind the sofa.

Mom gasped. "Naughty cat! Why aren't you in the basement?"

The cat batted the ball of yarn back and forth across the floor then began pulling the yarn loose with his mouth.

"Stop it! Give me that!" Mom grabbed the tangled ball of yarn and tugged. "Let go." She took a deep breath and blew in the cat's face.

Arrow dropped the yarn. Mom picked it up and winced. Damp strands hung limply from the ball. "Look what you did."

Arrow laid down at her feet. He lowered his head.

She set the yarn down. "You know, you'd be a pretty cat if you were brushed. Right now, you're a mess."

Arrow perked his ears then rubbed his head against her foot.

Without thinking, she scratched him behind the ears. Arrow didn't hesitate. He jumped up on her lap.

"It's not that I don't like you," Mom said. "We just don't have room for another pet." Her words faded as Arrow's purring grew louder.

She stroked his fur.

She rubbed his chin.

She even gave him a hug.

Mom forgot all about her knitting.

"You know, Arrow, I've thought about it," Mom said. "I think we can make room."

Carolyn Weisbecker is an online student at Southern New Hampshire University where she will earn her master's degree in English and Creative Writing in October. Carolyn writes children's middle grade novellas and short stories. She has been published in the *Penmen Review*, and in July, *The Mark Literary Review* will publish my story, *The Butterfly Killer.*

Illustration by **Lisa Wee**

Lisa Wee graduated from the University of Hertfordshire with 2nd class honors. Her work is quint, quirky and vibrant. She loves developing characters that embraced inclusive and multiculturalism. Living in a multicultural society allows her to be sensitive yet receptive to being "different" Her illustrations depicts adventurous, fun and multicultural children love being together.

Bennett Clement Jones: Bubble Cloud Creator

by Robert Holcomb III

Bennett hated the idea of starting over. A new home, new school, and his biggest fear, making new friends, occupied his thoughts as he stared out the window of his mother's car at the passing scenery. His mom had taken a new job across the country, and that meant leaving everything they knew and loved behind.

The small red car passed a sign: "Welcome to Alto Cumulous: Atmospheres Above Everyone Else." Bennett chuckled to himself at the sign. The little red car drove through the small downtown, with stores lined up on both sides of the main street. Residents of Alto Cumulous were out walking and enjoying the bright sunny day. The small red car drove on, and something caught Bennett's eye. A unique store that changed his sadness to happiness. The small store, next to the food shoppe, had a statue of a tuxedoed man standing on the roof. The tuxedoed man had a giant head compared to his body and stood behind a giant bottle labeled "Bubbles." As Bennett watched the giant man and giant bubble bottle, the bubble wand appeared out of the bottle, and the man blew a bubble down toward the small red car.

"Mom, did you see that? We have to check that store out!" Bennett said.

"We'll explore later. We have to meet the movers at our new house," Mom responded.

The small red car pulled up to a small white house just as the moving truck parked in the driveway. After the movers left, Bennett and his mom drove into town to buy groceries for dinner. The small red car parked in front of the Alto Cumulous Food Shoppe, and Bennett saw the giant tuxedoed man again. The unique store, which had the name, O'Dea's Purveyor of Unique Curios, stood next to the food shoppe. Bennett's mom told him he had fifteen minutes to go into the store, then meet her. Jumping with excitement, he ran for O'Dea's as his allowance jingled in his pocket. As he approached the sidewalk, a shower of bubbles fell around him.

Bennett entered the store, and a set of bells rang. The store had everything he had ever wanted; toy trains, oversized teddy bears, battery-powered planes suspended from the ceiling, flying in circles, and a surprise: an entire wall containing many bottles of bubbles. Bennett looked at the colorful bottles, mesmerized.

A small hand tapped him on his shoulder. Bennett made a small squeal in fright. A short woman with blue hair jumped back in surprise and chuckled. She smiled and greeted Bennett with a friendly "Hello."

Putting his hand to his chest, he felt his heart racing. "I apologize, ma'am. I was fascinated by all the colorful bottles!"

"It is quite impressive. No two bottles the same. Each one from a different part of the world," the woman said.

Bennett looked at her as though she were crazy. She smiled and picked up a scarlet bottle from the wall and placed it in his hands. The bottle was glass, and he read the name out loud:

"Harper's Bubbles of Valencia, Spain."

The woman spoke. "Each bottle of bubbles contains its own magic from a unique city. Not known to myself or the peddler I buy them from."

Bennett put Harper's Bubbles back on the shelf and picked up a cobalt-blue triangle-shaped bottle, Maverick's Bubbles of Rhyolite, Nevada. Bennett liked the names, and seeing and feeling the different bottle shapes. Names like Aggie's Bubbles of Cork, Ireland, Houston's Bubbles of Florence, Italy, Pepper's Bubbles—a black-as-night glass bottle—of Centralia, Pennsylvania. Then one bottle made Bennett stop and stare. An emerald-green bottle, bright and shiny, shaped like a Japanese pagoda. The bottle stood a little taller than the rest. Reading the name, Patterson's Bubbles of A Slumberous Mount, Idaho, Bennett's mouth fell open. The woman stood watching him stare at the green bottle, grinning.

"Are you alright?" She smiled again.

Bennett picked up and turned the bottle in his hands. The detail of the pagoda bottle was extraordinary. The doors, the windows, even the railings, were amazing.

Bennett turned and talked to the woman. "I am from A Slumberous Mount; we have a park with a Japanese pagoda, this exact pagoda, only bigger. How is this possible? I didn't know we made anything except potatoes."

A car horn sounded from outside, and Bennett realized he was late to meet his mother. It must have been more than fifteen minutes. He asked the woman if he could buy the bottle of Patterson's Bubbles. She put her hands around his as he held the bottle.

"Take this bottle as a welcome gift, Bennett. It holds a special meaning for you, and it seems the bottle has been waiting for you."

"Thank you, ma'am. I'm late meeting my mother. I need to go before I get into trouble."

The woman called to him. "Bennett, you have magic in your hands. Use it to conquer your fears."

Bennett smiled, left O'Dea's, and was just headed for the food shoppe when the strangest thought occurred to him. How did she know his name?

Bennett ran into the Alto Cumulous Food Shoppe and saw his mom at the cart corral. He looked and thought she was done with the shopping, but there were no bags.

Bennett's mom saw him running toward her, and she asked, "Were they closed?"

"I've been over there for half an hour. I'm sorry I'm late," Bennett responded, confused.

"Sweetie, I just walked in. Are you feeling OK? Are you coming down with a fever? Let me feel your forehead," she said jokingly as she reached for Bennett.

Bennett, still confused, told his mom he had no fever. He showed his mom the Patterson's Bubbles of A Slumberous Mount bottle with excitement as they walked toward the dairy section. Bennett continued his tale through the food shoppe as he described the many bottles. Bennett's mom smiled and listened to Bennett as the cashier bagged their groceries. They walked to the little red car, and Bennett still talked about bubble bottles.

The next day, Bennett left his house and walked to Cirrus Park, a few blocks away. Walking through the gate, he found a huge open space of green grass with few trees. There was a group of kids playing catch at the far side of the park. Bennett walked to an empty corner with his bottle of bubbles and sat under a big oak tree. Looking up at the sky, he saw many fluffy white clouds and immediately started making shapes with his imagination. One cloud took the shape of a cupcake complete with cherry. Another, bigger cloud resembled a giraffe.

Picking up the bottle, he unscrewed the lid and removed the wand. He blew gently to get as many bubbles from the wand as possible, and the bubbles floated out and away from him. Silently they drifted up toward the sky. Bennett put the wand in the bottle for a second batch. This time he let out a slow, long breath to make one giant bubble. The bubble had reached the size of his head when it broke free, floated away, dipped toward the grass, and swiftly flew up skyward. Bennett had just put the wand into the bottle for a third batch when something fell to his left.

Bennett turned his head and saw a small bird ... in a clear ball. The bird looked scared and confused, and it was flapping its wings. As Bennett looked at the ball with extreme curiosity, a shimmer of rainbow colors circled around it. "My bubble?"

He touched the bubble with his hand. Ripples appeared, frightening the bird more. Bennett took the wand and touched the bubble. The bubble popped, and the bird flew away. Bennett looked around the park and saw bubbles falling all over.

He jumped to his feet just as a bigger bubble landed. It was as tall as him. Bennett saw his reflection in the shiny surface. Inside the bubble, there appeared fluffy white cotton candy ... "CLOUDS!"

The cloud in the bubble resembled a cupcake with a cherry on the top. Bennett became giddy and ran around this "bubble cloud." Touching the cupcake bubble turned it every color he knew of under the sunlight. Then a shadow passed overhead. Another bubble, much bigger, was about to land.

With a deep thud, the bubble came to rest on the grass. Bennett stared at the massive bubble and realized it was taller than his house. A small breeze blew, and the bubble began to spin slowly. Inside was a cloud shaped like a giraffe. The bubble refracted the sunlight, and beams of color splashed over every inch of Cirrus Park. The kids in the park stopped playing and looked toward

Bennett and the bubble. The giraffe continued to spin, and beams of color spun, creating a mirror ball effect over the entire park.

The park kids walked to Bennett with much curiosity and asked about his bubble cloud creations. Bennett smiled and started talking to the park kids about his magic bubble bottle. All at once the kids stared up to the sky and made different shapes in the clouds. Bennett blew bubbles to capture the shapes his new friends saw. Once the bottle emptied, Bennett and his friends were in an ocean of colors and bubble creations that overflowed the Cirrus Park walls. Bennett and his new friends ran through the bubble collection, bouncing off the bubbles and laughing. They played tag and hide-and-seek.

By five o'clock Bennett and his friends were lying in the grass, looking up at the sky through the pile of shimmering bubbles, and smiling.

"I'm going to like it here."

Robert Holcomb III lives in San Francisco California. He has been writing and drawing children's stories for over ten years now and feels he has new ideas and twists on old ones that children would enjoy reading.

Tiny Mountain

By Laura Muncie

Some mountains are tiny. Don’t believe me?

To an ant a meatball is Mount Everest. But an ant can climb a meatball faster than you can eat one!

To a spider you are a T-Rex! But a spider is probably running up your pyjama leg right now.

Watch out!

Some mountains are invisible. You can't see them, but they are real.

Saturday is the worst day for a tiny invisible mountain to appear. That’s what happened at Leon’s house. It grew over the balcony, across the yard till Leon couldn’t see the park anymore.

When Leon's Dad said he should tidy his toys, the mountain got in the way!

When Leon’s friends asked him to be goalkeeper playing soccer, the mountain stood in the net.

When Leon’s Dad called him inside for dinner the mountain got bigger!

When Leon tried to eat his broccoli, the mountain sat on his plate and squashed his dinner!

Leon loved wearing a bubble beard in the bath, but not tonight! the mountain was in the bath.

Then the stars came out. Leon didn't want to go to bed, he wanted to stay on the balcony and star gaze.

'How will you manage to get into bed with a mountain in your room?' asked Leon's Mum smiling.

Leon didn't know. All day the mountain had followed him around. Stopping him doing things he wanted to do. Stopping him doing things he didn't want to do.

'Why don't you tell the mountain to go away?' Leon's Mum asked, looking up at the dark sky.

Telling a mountain to go away didn't sound easy to Leon.

'Every night the stars shine, even with mountains in front of them.' his Mum said.

Leon's Mum held him close. 'Mountains are real Leon, but you can shine brighter! Lift yourself up high. Like these stars.'

Leon padded through to the bathroom. The mountain was beside the sink. But Leon brushed his teeth anyway, and the mountain shrunk!

Then he wandered into his bedroom. Leon wasn't sure if there was room for him and the mountain in his bed.

Outside a large moon glowed, and stars winked.

Leon took one step towards the mountain, then another. The mountain got smaller.

Some toys were near the mountain, so Leon put them away. The mountain got even smaller!

Leon squeeze into his bed. The mountain lay beside him on his pillow.

Leon stretched out his arms and legs into a star shape.

'I can do it' he said yawning. 'I can shine like a star'.

Leon yawned again, and the mountain was gone.

Originally from Scotland, **Laura Muncie** has been living for the last 7 years in Germany. She is a journalist with a Scottish newspaper and teach English part time. Laura is married and has a lovely 4yr old boy, who is a source of joy and inspiration.

Illustration by **Laura Muncie**

Do Monkeys Cry?

By Aashi Parikh

Ahalya has been a monkey for most of her life. Her older sister moved to China when Ahalya was five and learnt Mandarin there, and when she came home to visit she named Ahalya Xiao Hotze. "Little monkey," she said, "That's what it means, and isn't that what you are?" Then she caught Ahalya and tickled her till she was gasping for air through her laughs. Her cousin called her a monkey too, teasing her for her naughty ways, climbing trees and walls and roofs and wreaking havoc. Over the years, many of her friends and schoolmates have also told her that she is a monkey – some jokingly, some meanly, some admiringly. It has been said enough times now for Ahalya to know with certainty – she is a monkey.

When Ahalya was a baby, her parents were not happy with each other. Their voices would echo through the house like wolves howling at the night or lions growling at their prey. Ahalya wanted them to stop, so she would cry, loud as a wailing shearwater. Have you heard a shearwater before? It is a funny seabird that makes a terribly loud crying call at night. Other shearwaters respond in a similar manner, but Ahalya's parents did not. So, she stopped crying.

Not long after, she became a monkey. First, she learnt to walk, then she learnt to climb. From then on, whenever she hears the raised, animal voices of her parents, she retreats up her favorite fig tree that rises from their front road, branching far over the electricity poles to the other side of the street. Ahalya can climb almost to the top, where the slimmest branches wave gently in the afternoon breeze, but she never goes all the way. She always stops several feet below, something holding her back.

Alone, sitting almost at the top of her tree, Ahalya usually feels safe. But today is different. Today her parents have been yelling for hours, and she does not know what animals they sound like anymore. Today Ahalya is scared and feels cold inside. She feels as though her world is slowly coming apart, and all she wants is to curl up and cry. Later in the afternoon, when her mother and father are in their bedroom, Ahalya sneaks to the computer and turns it on. This has become a habit lately – Ahalya is nine now and uses the computer frequently for schoolwork. She has learnt that she can ask it almost any question and it will answer her. Her parents do not answer all her questions nearly as readily as the internet, so she asks them less and less and turns more and more to the glowing screen in front of her. This time she types into the search bar carefully, "Do monkeys cry?"

No. Monkeys, all primates, and in fact all animals apart from humans do not cry.

Ahalya closes the computer screen and takes a deep breath. She walks outside and sits on the front steps, and her thoughts begin to wander. In her mind she is a little golden capuchin – she has read about them before, they are small monkeys that live in Brazil and sometimes the tribal folk there keep them as pets. Ahalya the monkey is not afraid of the thin topmost branches. She leaps fearlessly from tree to tree, effortlessly skimming over the canopy that covers their street. She continues past the street into a wild and dense forest that exists only in her imagination. Butterflies of every color come swirling out as she passes. A panther with golden eyes and a coat made of shadows moves stealthily below. A cloud of glittering fairies suddenly surrounded her and bear her up, up, up into the sky.

Then she is crossing the Sahara Desert, a sand viper snaking over the dunes beneath her. Then she is above the Pacific Ocean and schools of bottlenose dolphins leap out to greet her, chattering happily in whistles and clicks. "Ahalya," her mother calls from somewhere far away, but Ahalya does not hear. Now she has landed on the peak of Kanchenjunga, one of the world's tallest mountains, and snow blizzards all around her, settling in her fur and chilling her deep in her bones. The fairies have left her here and gone. "Ahalya," her mother stands behind her, calling her name again, and Ahalya returns to the front steps. "Yes Ma," she says. Her mother asks if she is okay, and when Ahalya nods yes, she tells her to come inside and help with dinner. Ahalya stands up. It is such an ordinary request, as though this is a normal evening like any other, that Ahalya is quite happy to oblige. But though the day is warm, the chill from the mountain snow has not quite left her bones, and it holds on to her insides, telling her that everything is not what it seems.

Ahalya stands kneading dough in the kitchen while her mother chops vegetables next to her and her father lays the table. They are each there in the same space within a few feet of each other, yet the distance between them seems as vast as if they were on separate continents. Ahalya feels something building inside her – something big and overwhelming. She shivers and tries to shake it off. She imagines a swarm of bumblebees whirring madly in her stomach and lungs and intestine, all trying to fly out. She imagines her ribs coated with frost that cages her heart. She imagines a fraying rope which anchors her to her parents, coming undone. She does not know how to ask her parents what is happening, and she is afraid she is about to cry so she runs out of the kitchen, out the door, onto the street and up her tree.

There she sits, shaking and terrified.

She wants to go rushing back to her mother and father and break down and let them comfort her, let them tell her they love her and that everything will be okay. But she knows this will not happen. If she cries they will not listen and another layer of frost will coat her heart. Monkeys do not cry. To cry is to hurt more, she will not do it. Monkeys do not cry. Monkeys run free.

Ahalya is startled from her thoughts by the sound of leaves rustling loudly and the quivering of branches around her. Suddenly, her father's head appears next to her knee, and then the rest of his body. He pulls himself up beside her and makes himself comfortable. Ahalya is too shocked to say anything. What is he doing here?

Mr. Rose, Ahalya's father, looks his daughter straight in the face and takes her hand. For a few moments, he is quiet. Then, gazing out over the street he says, "Do you remember the first time you tried to climb this tree? You were only two. You stood up on my shoulders and grabbed the lowest branch, laughing like a hyena, and then your mother and I helped you sit on it." Ahalya shakes her head, she has no memory of this, although she has been climbing her tree as long as she can remember. Mr. Rose smiles gently at her, "Come down, Ahalya." She does not know what else to do, so she follows him back to the ground below. She thinks she can hear the fairies whispering to each other from above, but she ignores them.

Mrs. Rose is standing at the bottom of the tree, her apron covered with flour and falling off one shoulder. As soon as she sees Ahalya she pulls her into a deep, enveloping hug. The frost inside Ahalya does not know what to do with all this warmth, so it begins to melt and, unable to stop herself, the tears come flowing out from Ahalya's eyes, soaking her mother's apron, then moving through her body in giant sobs. "Oh, my sweetheart," Ahalya's mother says softly into her hair, tears beading like diamonds in her own eyes. Mr. and Mrs. Rose guide their daughter back towards the house, and they all sit down together on the front steps. Mr. Rose has his arms around both of them, like a father gorilla protecting his family. Family. They feel like a family in that moment, and because Ahalya has been craving this feeling with such hunger for so long without even knowing it, she senses all the bumblebees escaping and all her insides thawing, and she has no way to hold the tears in.

When the sobs of both mother and daughter quieten, Mr. Rose begins to tell a story. He says that when he was a very young boy, he lived on a farm with his parents and grandparents and they owned many acres of apple orchards. In Fall, when the apple season would begin, he and his brothers would race each other to see who could gather the most apples. He would always win because he was the quickest and lightest, and he could always climb the highest. He says that when he grew up into a young man, he met a beautiful girl, and on their first date together he took her on a picnic. She was wearing a lacy white frock that day, but when they sat to eat lunch under an oak tree, the first thing she did was clap her hands with joy, throw off her slippers, and go climbing up its branches. The girl was Mrs. Rose, and he fell in love with her at that very moment. He continues the story, talking about his daughter, how he has watched her grow over the years, living in her own world, always more at home in her tree. At the end, he hugs them both tighter and says to Ahalya, "My little monkey, you are not alone. Do you see? We are a family of monkeys."

Ahalya is so astounded at this analogy, at the idea that her mother and father could be monkeys like her, that she bursts out laughing. Mr. Rose pokes his wife playfully and says, "She doesn't believe me! Looks like you'll just have to prove it to her." And Mrs. Rose stands, pulling her daughter up with her. The three of them walk back to the tree. The evening has grown dark, but the streetlights are on, and there is a wonderful feeling of lightness around them. Mrs. Rose looks radiant. Something has changed, something has healed. Ahalya imagines the fraying rope of before wounding thick with new, shining threads. Now her parents have begun to make monkey noises, and all three of them giggling at their own silliness, they climb the tree one after the other. This time Ahalya scurries up higher than she has ever been, past the fear, right to the top.

The bees are out. The frost is gone. The sky is studded with stars, or maybe it is just the fairies gone far for a while to gift Ahalya this moment. Monkeys do not cry, the internet said, but it was wrong. Monkeys cry, and then they look after each other, and then they laugh. Ahalya has always known that she is a monkey, but only now does she know that her parents are too. They have not said aloud to her that everything will be okay, and maybe it won't, maybe this is just a calm before new storms begin to brew. But the word family holds them tightly together in this gifted moment, and somehow Ahalya knows – it will endure.

Aashi Parikh is a marine biologist and an occasional writer and poet. She usually writes about whales and dolphins, but this story is about a monkey.

Illustration by **Annaleigha Wilke**

Annaleigha Wilke is a Master's student working on her final thesis, and her interests lie in children's education and stories, the 1800s, monsters and happy moments. She enjoys playing with her adopted ferrets, gardening and traveling whenever she has the chance.

The Boy With the Inner Voice

by Adrian Hardy Hansen

The little boy could hear the other kids as they screamed, laughed and played around in the background. He would stand there, looking at them with envy, but he never dared to join in.

Each day would pass, and he wouldn't speak, all he did was listen to the little voice in his head. It was so smart, it knew everything - it could read their minds.

As the little boy would pass a person in the hallway, the little voice would tell him what they thought:

"You're stupid", "You're weird", "Don't look at me", and the little boy would listen to it. His eyes would fall towards the floor as he swiftly pulled them away from whomever they fell on, and he would reply to the voice:

"Okay, I won't talk to anyone, I won't look at anyone. Nobody likes me", but what the little boy didn't want to admit, is that the truth bothered him - that it made him sad. He hated this voice - he hated listening to it.

Each recess, he would stand in the corner, as far away from everyone else as possible, just so his voice wouldn't talk to him. And if someone walked towards him, he would quickly look away while avoiding eye-contact, just to let them know he wants to be alone.

The little boy - convinced that the voice spoke the truth - believed it. He thought that he was stupid, he thought that he was weird - that people didn't want to be friends with him. He started looking at himself in the mirror, saying to himself:

"You're ugly", and the next day, while passing a person in the hallway, the voice would say to him:

"You're ugly. You're stupid. You're weird", and he would believe it, thinking it spoke the truth. But what the little boy didn't realize, is that the voice in his head didn't exist - it was nothing but his thoughts. He, himself, thought that he was ugly - that he was weird, stupid and friendless.

There was no voice, there was no mind-reading - nobody else then him believed it. The boy he passed in the hallway didn't think he was ugly, nor stupid or weird; the girl walking up to him in recess didn't think he was ugly, stupid or weird - it was just him. He, himself, thought that he was ugly - that he was weird, stupid and friendless, and now that he knew, he started looking at himself in the mirror, saying to himself:

"You're cool."

He would wake up every morning, and say to himself:

"You're funny."

When he handed in his homework, and his teacher told him he was smart, he would say to himself:

"You're smart."

And now, when he passed a person in the hallway, his voice would tell him:

"You're cool You're funny You're smart", and the boy would smile as he walked along with his friends.

Adrian Hardy Hansen is 19-year-old, living in Norway and spending a year between studies, writing, working etc. His favorite author is Knut Hamsun, favorite composer is Frédéric Chopin and favorite place is Sørøya, Norway.

Illustration by **Mirela Mandžo**

Mirela Mandžo is from Tuzla, Bosnia and Herzegovina. She is 22 years old and she is a student of geography. Her interest in drawings started when she was just 3 years old, and every free moment she dedicates to children illustration art.

CPSIA information can be obtained
at www.ICGtesting.com
Printed in the USA
LVHW071728171219
640668LV00033B/1434/P